AUTUMN'S DAWN

D1371262

KIM SIGAFUS

7th GENERATION
Summertown, Tennessee

Library of Congress Cataloging-in-Publication Data
available upon request.

Cover and interior design: John Wincek

7th Generation
Book Publishing Company
PO Box 99, Summertown, TN 38483
888-260-8458
bookpubco.com
nativevoicesbooks.com

ISBN: 978-1-939053-25-1

25 24 23 22 21 20   1 2 3 4 5 6 7 8 9

> We can only be what we give
> ourselves the power to be.
>
> **NATIVE PROVERB**

This book is dedicated to everyone still searching for their true self, and who, in the process, will discover the power to effect change in their own lives and in the lives of others.

CONTENTS

AUTUMN'S DAWN

Happy Reunion

Autumn sighed. With a jolt, her head hit the truck's window for the third time. She rubbed the painful spot and then adjusted the small blanket she had propped up against the window. Her mother had packed the blanket, as well as several other items, in her duffel bag for the trip, and she had promptly taken it out as soon as she had gotten into the rickety old truck. She closed her eyes, trying to block out the sun that was shining in through the windows, and yawned. It had already been a long day.

Her father, Tom, was sprawled out next to her, driving. He had picked her up very early that morning and had waited somewhat impatiently for Autumn to get ready. Now he was weaving in and out of traffic as he passed cars with boats hitched to them heading for the lake in the other direction.

They had been on the road for what seemed like forever. Autumn knew they had at least an hour

1

to go before they arrived in Minneapolis and got to Aunt Jessie's apartment. She clutched the duffel bag she had refused to put in the back seat and sat up now, letting the blanket drop into her lap.

"Are we there yet?" she asked, her mouth twitching as she tried not to smile.

"Yup . . . get out."

Autumn grinned and then laughed. She knew he would say that. They were going about sixty miles an hour down the highway at the moment.

It was a game they started playing when she was a child, and it always made her laugh. She glanced out the window and then shook her head.

"Ah, no thank you," she replied with a grin. "But, Dad, I have to go to the bathroom."

He sighed and shook his head. "I just passed several places to go," he replied, frowning over at her. You'll have to wait until we get to the next town."

"When's that?"

"About twenty minutes or so."

"Okay. So can we get something to eat there too?"

Tom shook his head. "Your aunt has lunch waiting for you."

"I'm hungry."

Tom smiled. "If I know my sister, she'll have plenty of food. She is so excited you're coming."

"I wish I could stay longer."

"Me too. But you have to get back for tutoring or you won't pass this year."

Autumn grimaced. "I worked as hard as I could . . ."

"I know," interrupted her father, putting on his blinker to pass someone. "But they discovered your dyslexia too late in the year." He sighed. "I wish you had said something earlier."

"I was embarrassed. I didn't want anyone to know how stupid I was."

Tom took his eyes off the road to glance at her for a moment, then moved his gaze back to the road.

"You're not stupid, Autumn. Am I stupid? I'm dyslexic too."

When Autumn didn't answer, he sighed. "Look, I think the best thing to do is let the school help you. The tutoring staff will teach you different ways to learn, and school will hopefully become easier for you."

"I guess."

"Oh, hang on. I forgot about this gas station. Let's pull in here to use the bathroom and get a drink."

Tom pulled into the large gas station parking lot as Autumn finally threw her backpack into the back seat.

Ten minutes later they were back on the road again. Autumn pulled her music out and put her earbuds in. Prince's music came through them, and she closed her eyes.

As she sat back, her thoughts returned to the last couple of months. School had gone better as the teachers worked with her more, but she hadn't caught up by the end of the year. She was given a week off, and after that she had to go back for two weeks of tutoring. If she did well with the tutoring, they would pass her into the next grade.

She wasn't the only one going back, though. She'd heard that Sydney, the girl who had bullied her all last school year, was also going to have to attend. Autumn wondered what Sydney's father thought about that. He was a tough man to like.

She and Sydney hadn't spoken after the Jingle Dress play they did in the spring, but she'd heard rumors about Sydney's parents breaking up. The girl had become very quiet toward the end of the year, and Autumn felt sorry for her. Sydney and her friends had stopped bothering Autumn for the moment, and she was glad for that.

Autumn opened her eyes to glance over at her father. He had been making regular visits to the house to see her and Sam, Autumn's baby brother. Sometimes her mom was there and sometimes she was at work, but it was always prearranged. Even though her father was trying to make things work with her mother, they weren't as close as he would like them to be. Her mother told him she was not ready to reconcile. She had started to date other people, which had not made her father very happy. He was still holding out for his happy ending, which included having Autumn's mother and his family back. But Autumn's mother was obviously ready to move on.

Autumn had watched her mother blossom into a more independent woman in the last couple of months. She had taken over almost all the chores Autumn had been doing and was more present in everyone's lives. Autumn was proud of her and told her so. That being said, she didn't know how she felt about her mother dating. Autumn was aware of the wistful smiles when her mother returned home from the dates. She was enjoying herself and dating made her happy, which Autumn was in full support of. When Autumn asked her mother about the dates, she replied that she was keeping things casual, and Autumn had left it at that.

Autumn moved her gaze back to the window and drifted off to sleep a few minutes later. After an hour or so, her father gave her a quick poke as they pulled into the parking lot of Jessie's apartment building.

"We're here," he said as he put the truck in park. Autumn sat up sleepily and pushed her hair back out of her face.

They were sitting in front of a large brick apartment complex that consisted of several buildings. There were flower gardens scattered around, and even a fountain with a statue of a little girl holding an umbrella. Water was shooting up through the umbrella handle and coming out the top to rain down on the open umbrella.

"This place looks rich," muttered Autumn, grabbing her backpack out of the back seat.

"Jessie likes to be in the center of things," replied her father getting out of the car. "This neighborhood has great shopping and restaurants. They also have specialty shops, and she has some beadwork in them for sale."

"Really? That's cool."

"I think so too. Oh, there's your aunt now, waving at us." He pointed to his right, and there was Jessie, waving her hands and running toward them. A smile broke across Autumn's face, and she dropped her backpack and ran to meet her.

"Oh, I am so happy to see you," said Jessie, hugging Autumn tightly. "You have grown at least a foot since I last saw you."

Autumn beamed as her father strode up and gave his sister a hug.

"Boozoo, little brother," Jessie said with a grin. "Long time, no see."

Tom grimaced and shook his head. "You just saw me yesterday. And when are you moving back to the rez? This is a long trip."

Jessie shook her head. "You make it all the time. And my life is here now."

"Our people are nomadic."

"*Some* of our people are nomadic," she answered. "I am not."

Autumn went over to the truck, picked up her backpack, and followed her father as Jessie led them inside.

Her aunt's apartment was big, with white walls and colorful furniture. A tidy place, it had Native paintings covering the walls and some of Jessie's beadwork tapestries as well. She had a large balcony overlooking the fountain. Autumn opened the sliding glass door and stepped outside. The whole place was beautiful, and Autumn understood why Jessie was not eager to move back to the reservation.

"It's a whole different world here," said Autumn. "I can hear cars and truck noise, honking horns, and people laughing and talking on the other balconies. It's a different kind of sociable here."

"I'm leaving," announced her father a few moments later.

"What? Why?" asked Autumn, turning from the outside view. "You're not eating lunch with us?"

"I have to get to work," he replied. "I picked up an extra shift today."

"Well, let me at least pack food up for you," said Jessie, and she got busy doing so.

"Okay, well, thanks for bringing me here," said Autumn.

Tom nodded, walking outside to join her. "I will return next Saturday afternoon. Your mom is expecting you home at a reasonable time."

Autumn nodded. "I think she has a date, and I need to babysit."

A shadow fell over Tom's face. "Yeah." He sighed. "I wish things were different," he grumbled.

Autumn hesitated a moment and then replied, "I just want her to be happy. She was unhappy for such a long time."

Tom nodded. "I know. I want that for her too. I just wish she could be happy with me and not some other guy. I really blew it when I left."

"I'm sorry, Dad."

"Yeah, me too."

Tom gave Autumn a kiss on the forehead and headed back inside. He grabbed the bag of food from his sister and then headed for the door. He pulled it open, then turned to smile and wave before he headed to his truck.

Jessie caught the unhappy look on Autumn's face, and she went to give her a hug.

"There's nothing you can do about it," she reminded her. "Those two will have to figure things out on their own. You have your own life to lead."

"I know."

"Now, let's eat," said Jessie, pulling back to smile at her. "I want to hear all about what's been happening at school."

Autumn smiled and followed her to the table. She took a banana and started to peel it. She took a bite and closed her eyes, savoring the taste. She loved bananas.

Five minutes later, the doorbell rang. Autumn was just starting to fill her plate when her aunt got up to answer it.

Jessie pulled the door open with a grin. "What did you forget now, Tom? Oh, it's you. I didn't expect you today, Ryan."

"I know," he replied. "I took a chance you might be home. I thought maybe we could go to Como Zoo."

"Oh, I'm sorry. I have my niece for the week and . . ."

"Zoo? I love the zoo," said Autumn.

She came around the corner to see a tall blond man with green eyes standing just inside the door of the apartment. His wavy hair was cut short, and he wore jeans and a tucked-in, short-sleeved, button-down brown shirt.

"Hello," he said with a smile. "I'm Ryan. I'm a friend of Jessie's."

"Friend?"

"Well, I would like to think of myself as her boyfriend, but she likes to play the field," he answered with a grin, and Jessie shook her head.

"You can stop talking about me as if I wasn't here," she said, giving him a stern look. "And we are dating."

"We have been *dating* for two years," he pointed out. "I would like us to move ahead, but Jessie's as slow as a turtle when it comes to those things."

Autumn grinned. "Well, it is nice to meet you. We were just sitting down for lunch. Would you like to join us?"

Ryan gave Jessie a smile. "I would love to."

"Autumn, don't encourage him," whispered Jessie, pushing the door shut as he walked in and rounded the corner to the dining room.

"It doesn't seem like he needs too much encouragement," Autumn whispered back. "And he is cute."

"Cute? When did you start noticing boys?"

"Just now."

Jessie laughed. "Okay, girl. Get a hold of yourself. Let's get back to the table before he eats everything in sight. You don't know what you've done inviting him to lunch."

"Are you mad about it? I probably should have asked first."

"No, it's okay."

Autumn sat down next to Ryan, and Jessie sat across from them. As Ryan caught Jessie's eye, he winked, and she blushed and looked away.

Autumn hid a grin as she reached over to grab a biscuit. No, it didn't seem like Jessie minded Ryan being here one bit.

CHAPTER 2

Trust Issues

The three of them talked as Ryan took some meat and cheese and started making his sandwich from the fixings Jessie had laid out. Autumn finished making her sandwich and glanced over in surprise as Ryan stopped and leaned his arms on the table to regard Jessie seriously.

"So when are you going to marry me? I'm not getting any younger, and neither are you."

Autumn dropped her butter knife with a clatter, and Jessie glanced from Autumn to Ryan, her face turning red.

"This is not the time to talk about that," hissed Jessie. "Just eat."

Ryan sat back and laid his hand over his chest with a grin. "But I'm pining away for you, and you're taking forever to make up your mind. When will I get an answer?" he asked playfully.

"When I have one to give you."

Jessie picked up two pieces of bread and spread them out on her plate, ignoring the indignant sputtering coming from Ryan.

"How long am I supposed to wait for you, may I ask?"

Jessie started laying pickles and onions over her ham slices and shook her head.

"If you're in that much of a hurry," she replied, "then don't wait."

"Excuse me?"

"I am not going to be pressured into anything."

"But I asked you last month. You would think by now . . ."

"Well, I have a lot of things to consider."

"Like what? You love me. I love you. Let's get married and have some kids."

"How do you even know I want them?"

"Well, do you?"

A silence fell over the table for a moment. No one moved or spoke, and Autumn squirmed in her chair, wishing she could figure out a way to remove herself from the room.

Jessie bit her lip and glanced over at Autumn. "I'm sorry about this, honey." She glanced over at Ryan, who was watching her, waiting for an answer. She sighed. "If this is how today is going to go, I think you should leave."

"But Jessie, I was only kidding . . . well, mostly kidding, anyway."

"Ryan."

Jessie stared at him but didn't say anything more. Surprised, Ryan blinked a few times and then nodded, pushing his chair back. The conversation started off playful enough, and he hadn't meant to even start this conversation with Autumn there, but it had all tumbled out of his emotional bucket, and now he couldn't figure out a way to shove it all back in there.

"I'm sorry," he said, glancing from Autumn to Jessie. "I never meant to make anyone uncomfortable."

He stood up and shoved his hands in his pockets as he started to move, then turned back to glance at Jessie again. "I love you, Jess. But if I'm not what you want, then do us both a favor and cut me loose."

When she didn't respond, he turned around and left, closing the door softly behind him.

Jessie's eyes teared up as she watched him leave. When the door clicked shut, she cleared her throat and continued making her sandwich. For a moment, no one spoke.

Autumn sighed. It seemed like she was surrounded by adults who couldn't make up their minds about anything. Jessie looked over at her and saw that Autumn was shaking her head.

"What?" she asked defensively.

"What's the matter with you?"

"Excuse me?"

"Go after him."

"You don't understand."

"Yes, I do. He was joking and hit a nerve or something. What's the problem? Are you scared or just stubborn?"

"That's disrespectful, Autumn, and you don't know what you're talking about. You're too young . . ."

"No, I'm not," interrupted Autumn. "Everyone around me seems to think that. Can't anyone see that I'm growing up? I understand what's going on around me."

Autumn sighed and then looked down at the table. "You're all afraid. My parents and now you. You're all afraid of being hurt. But you can't stand in one place for the rest of your life. You have to try to make things work with someone or let them go."

Jessie put her hand on Autumn's. "You're talking about your mother, aren't you?"

Autumn nodded. "And my father may have to let her go and move on. Why can't they figure this out?"

"It's easier for people on the outside to see what's happening to others on the inside," answered Jessie. "Sometimes we need to be told what we can't see."

"Yeah, I guess."

Jessie sighed, pulling her hand away. "Or refuse to see," she muttered.

"The people in this family sure have trust issues," remarked Autumn, and to her surprise, Jessie laughed.

"I guess that's so," replied Jessie. Then she glanced over at Autumn. "You, too, honey?"

"Well, I don't have good examples around me when it comes to stuff like that."

Jessie nodded. "I suppose not."

They finished up lunch and put away the leftovers. Autumn wanted to see some of the neighborhood, so they headed out to Jessie's car. As they rounded the corner of the apartment building, there was Ryan, leaning against his SUV.

"I couldn't leave," he said, gazing into Jessie's eyes. "I've been trying to get the courage to go back to the apartment."

Jessie glanced at Autumn, who nodded and gave her a look. Her gaze went back to Ryan.

"I'm sorry for what happened in the apartment," she said, and he smiled.

Pulling her into his arms, he kissed her, and Autumn turned away and grinned. Then he opened the car doors with his key fob, and they all settled into the plush seats.

Ryan turned the vehicle around and headed for the zoo. When Ryan reached out for Jessie's hand, she gave it to him, and Autumn leaned back in her seat and smiled.

CHAPTER 3

Girl Time

Autumn woke up to complete silence. For a moment she didn't know where she was. Then, as she looked around the room, she remembered.

Sitting up, she yawned and then slid out of bed. She walked barefoot into the living room and found her aunt putting the finishing touches on breakfast.

Jessie looked at Autumn's purple pajamas and smiled.

"I like that color," she said, and Autumn nodded.

"It's my new favorite color," Autumn said, sitting down to watch Jessie pull the toast out of the toaster.

"I was just going to come and wake you," said Jessie. "We have a busy day ahead of us."

"What are we going to do?"

"Well, I have some craftwork I am going to bring over to the store that carries my work," answered Jessie, putting a plate of food in front of her. "I have to be there by ten this morning."

"Okay."

"And then I am heading out to gather willow branches for my dream-catcher orders."

"People order them from you? That's cool."

"I think so too. Then, after that, we are headed to the Miller Farmer's Market to do a little shopping."

"I like shopping."

"I know you do."

"Will Ryan be joining us?"

"No."

Autumn bit into her toast and regarded Jessie seriously. "I like him," she declared, and Jessie smiled.

"Me too."

"You gonna marry him?"

"Probably. But I'm not going to let him push me into picking a date."

"You're going to go down fighting, huh?"

Jessie shot her a look, and Autumn laughed.

"Man, I would be shopping for a big, beautiful dress and picking out my colors, and music, and flowers, and . . ."

Jessie grinned. "Slow down there, girl. I haven't even told him I would marry him yet. And you're too young to think about getting married. It's a huge commitment, you know."

"Yes, I know." Autumn reached over to take a banana out of the red ceramic bowl. "I don't even have a boyfriend."

"I didn't know you were interested in boys."

Autumn shrugged. "They're all right."

"Well, that's new. Is there anyone you like?"

Autumn shrugged. "Maybe."

"Maybe?" Jessie hurriedly pulled up a chair and sat down next to her niece. "Come on, let's hear about him. Tell me everything."

Autumn laughed. "Okay. Well, he just moved here. I saw him in the office when Mom and I went to sign up for summer school. We went in because Mom wanted to be sure there was going to be somebody in summer school who could help me specifically with my dyslexia."

"I see. That sounds smart."

"Yup. Anyway, he was at the counter when we got there, talking to the school secretary."

"And?"

"And I didn't catch his name."

"What does he look like?"

"He's tall and has long black hair, down to his waist."

"What makes him stand out from all the other Native guys around there?" asked Jessie.

"Well, for one thing, he has blue eyes. He caught me looking at him and smiled before he looked away. He seemed shy."

"Well, he is the new kid."

"Yeah, I guess. Anyway, I don't remember what his mother said his address is, but he is a townie."

"A what?"

"You know, someone who lives in oodena."

"Oodena? You mean in town?"

"Yeah, you know, instead of the country."

"I see. So you like this guy, huh?"

"I guess. I mean, I don't know him and probably won't see him until the next school year starts."

"Maybe you'll see him around oodena." Jessie stared at her for a moment and then asked, "Autumn, why do you mash sentences with Ojibwa words and English?"

Autumn shrugged. "I always have. Dad spoke a lot of Ojibwa, and Mom doesn't know much of the language." She grinned. "You know, when I was a baby, people thought I had a speech problem because they couldn't understand me at all. Not only do I have trouble with the s sound, but I was mashing languages together pretty early on. Dad finally realized that I could pick up a word or two of Ojibwa, and that's when they figured it out."

"I didn't know that." Jessie grinned. "You are a unique person, Autumn Dawn."

"Some people would say I'm weird."

Jessie shook her head. "No one that counts."

They finished their breakfast, and half an hour later they were heading to the shop that sells Jessie's items. Then they took a walk around Lake of the Isles and had lunch nearby. When they finished lunch, Jessie drove Autumn to downtown Minneapolis, where they did some shopping. By the time they returned to the apartment, they were exhausted.

"I think we should take it easy tomorrow," remarked Jessie, plopping her bags on the sofa and dropping into an overstuffed chair to remove her sandals. "I'm tired out."

"Me too," replied Autumn, leaning against the wall to remove her moccasins. "But I had so much fun."

"I don't feel much like cooking," said Jessie. "How about we order a pizza and have it delivered?"

"I'm up for that," replied Autumn. "How long will it take to get here? I'm hungry."

Jessie laughed. "Again? Girl, I have never seen anyone eat so much."

Autumn sat down on the other end of the couch, tucking her feet under her.

"Maybe I should be watching my weight," she said thoughtfully, glancing down at herself. "No guy will look at me if I am fat."

"You're not fat. You're just right. Not too big, not too little."

"You think so?"

"Just stay active," advised Jessie. "As women age, our bodies change. If you're worried about it, you could join some sports next year."

Autumn shook her head. "I'm not that into sports."

"Well, what do you like to do?"

"Most of the stuff I like to do requires sitting. Beadwork, sewing, reading . . ."

"I get that," interrupted Jessie, "but then you have to make time for physical activity. Maybe plan to take a walk every day. You still walk home from school, right?"

"Yes, but Mom is thinking about teaching me to drive."

"I would put that off for a while. If you have a license, you won't want to walk anywhere."

"But I want to get my license."

"Why? Where do you plan to go?"

"To the lake. Any time I want."

"The lake? Which lake?"

"Any of them. There are plenty in the area."

"There are plenty in Minnesota." Jessie thought for a moment. "Maybe your mom needs help running errands and that's why she wants you to get your license. But you can still find ways to keep active. I do a lot of walking."

"With Ryan?"

"Sometimes, but mostly by myself."

"It sounds lonely."

"Sometimes it is."

"Maybe you should get a dog."

"I can't have one here."

"Are you always going to live here? Maybe you should buy a house. Then you can get a dog."

"I probably will someday."

Autumn grinned. "After you marry Ryan?"

Jessie shook her head and then laughed. "You're as pushy as he is. Come on, let's go order that pizza."

As they got up, the doorbell rang. Jessie shot Autumn a glance, and Autumn grinned.

"I wonder who that is," she said innocently, and Jessie's eyes narrowed.

"If I didn't know better, I would think you called him," Jessie said. "But I know you don't have his number."

Autumn shrugged. "I have no idea who's at the door. But if it's Ryan, I don't mind. He's cute."

Jessie laughed. "Now wait a minute, young lady. He's mine, you know."

"Is he? You'd better snatch him up quickly then." Autumn made a great show of patting her hair into place. "Do you think he'd go for someone younger?"

Jessie picked up a pillow and threw it at her. Autumn ducked and it hit the lamp, knocking it over. They both laughed, and Autumn righted the lamp as Jessie went to the door.

Jessie pulled the door open and paused, eyeing Ryan and Tom with confusion.

"What are you two doing here?" she asked.

Ryan glanced at Tom and then leaned down to give her a quick kiss on the mouth. He brought his other hand out from behind him and thrust a bouquet of wildflowers at her.

"I've come to court you," he said with a grin, and Tom shook his head and rolled his eyes.

Jessie laughed. "So you came with my brother to do that?"

"Ah, no," said Tom, crossing his arms. "We both got here at the same time. I have nothing to do with the craziness standing next to me."

Jessie grinned and stepped aside so both men could enter the apartment. They walked into the living room, and Autumn stared at them with surprise.

"Dad, what are you doing here? Hi, Ryan."

Ryan nodded as Tom shoved his hands in his pockets.

"I'm here because I have the night off. I thought I would take you guys out to dinner," said Tom. He glanced over at Ryan. "But I see you have other plans."

"We have no other plans," said Autumn.

"No, I didn't know Ryan was coming over," said Jessie.

"Why don't you join us, Ryan?" asked Autumn. "Would that be okay, Dad?"

"I guess so," Tom replied.

Ryan grinned at Jessie. "I would love to, as long as it's okay with Jess."

Everyone looked over to see Jessie shrug. "It's fine with me. I'm not paying. But aren't you usually at the clinic late?"

"I got Dr. Whitehead to cover for me," replied Ryan. "I covered for him last month."

"Are you a doctor?" asked Autumn.

"He's a veterinarian," answered her father, and Ryan nodded.

"Yup, I work mostly with domestic animals, but occasionally I get a call for exotic ones."

"He's an emergency and critical care veterinarian," added Jessie. "So he's on call a lot."

"Wow, I didn't know there was such a thing," said Autumn. "I like animals. Maybe I could go to school for something like that."

"We can talk about it over dinner if you like," offered Ryan.

"Okay, that would be great."

Jessie and Autumn put their shoes back on while Ryan waited. They decided Tom would drive, so he went out to get the car. A few minutes later, Ryan escorted the women downstairs and into the waiting vehicle.

As Autumn hopped into the front seat, Ryan pulled Jessie toward him for a long kiss that left her blushing. Tom and Autumn grinned as the two broke apart and got into the back seat. Tom reached over for his daughter's hand and gave it a pat as he pulled out of the parking lot.

Bad and Good News

The week Autumn spent with her aunt went by fast, and before she knew it, Friday arrived. Autumn knew her father would be picking her up early the next morning, so she started to pack up some of her things that were strewn about the spare bedroom Jessie had given her to use.

In some ways, she was really sad to be leaving, but she did miss home and her mother and brother. Jessie told her she would try to come out again for Thanksgiving and that Autumn could call her any time she wanted to talk. Autumn appreciated that, as she had the feeling that spending part of the summer with Sydney was not going to be any fun.

The dinner with her father and Ryan had gone well, but neither of them had shown up again during the week. Autumn thought perhaps they were staying out of the picture to give her and Jessie some time together, and she was glad about that.

She loved getting to know her aunt better and felt even closer to her than ever. Watching her live her own life here in the city, away from the reservation, gave Autumn a chance to see another side of her. Jessie was a strong, independent woman with a great career in the arts, but she was also vulnerable and unsure of herself where Ryan was concerned. It helped Autumn realize that Aunt Jessie wasn't perfect and that she also made mistakes. That made Autumn feel better about herself and how she was handling her own life.

Autumn had been pleasantly surprised to discover how well known and respected her aunt was for her beadwork. She hoped that one day she would be able to make a living doing something that made her happy too.

"Autumn, supper is ready," her aunt called out, effectively interrupting Autumn's thoughts. "I hope you like soup."

Autumn came into the kitchen and frowned. "Soup in the summer? Mom only makes that when it's cold out."

"Well, it's an old family recipe," replied Jessie, filling two bowls up to the brim. "I wanted you to try it."

"Oh, okay."

Autumn sat down at the table, and Jessie brought over two bowls of steaming hot soup.

Autumn picked up her spoon and dipped it into the bowl. She blew on the soup before carefully putting it in her mouth and swallowing down the creamy mixture.

"Wow! This is really good," she said, digging into the bowl for another spoonful. "This is a family recipe?"

"Yup. I will send it home with you. Maybe you can make it for your family."

"Sounds good to me. Is it hard to make?"

"No, but there's a lot of prep involved."

"I don't mind that," replied Autumn. "I like to cook."

"I know. You are a good cook, too. Maybe that's where your calling is."

"What do you mean?"

Jessie smiled. "After you graduate, maybe you could go to a cooking school."

Autumn laughed. "I don't know about that. I'm not a very good student."

"Nonsense. You would be a great cook or chef or baker."

"But there's math involved," Autumn pointed out. "All that measuring and adding and subtracting and stuff."

"You're good at math," Jessie said. "Won't you be tutoring Sydney in math?"

Autumn's spoon stopped in midair. "What?"

"Oops. I probably wasn't supposed to tell you that," muttered Jessie with a sigh.

"What are you talking about?"

"Your mother called this morning. She wanted to find out what time Tom was getting you back home tomorrow."

"And?"

"And she mentioned that the tutoring teacher had called and said she was going to try something new this summer. She thought she would pair kids together who could help each other out with certain subjects, and she would be the support behind that."

"Why would she pair Sydney with me?"

"Well, it seems the girl is having math issues, and you are having English issues. She thought you could help each other get caught up."

"But me and Sydney? Is she crazy? Doesn't she know what happened last year? Which teacher is it?"

"She's new."

"Apparently," said Autumn, rolling her eyes.

Jessie frowned. "That's enough, Autumn. She deserves some respect. She is your teacher."

"I guess." Autumn set her spoon down and looked away.

This was absolutely terrible news. It was going to be the worst two weeks of her life.

"Why didn't Mom tell her not to put me with her?" asked Autumn quietly. She shook her head. "I don't understand. She is supposed to be protecting me from that stuff. She's throwing me right into Sydney's line of fire."

"Well, that's a little dramatic, don't you think?" asked Jessie before starting to eat again. "It's just two weeks of tutoring. Surely you two have grown up enough to put that stuff aside and get the work done to pass into the next grade. You don't want to be held back, do you?"

"No, I guess not."

"You can do this, Autumn. It's only two weeks. Work hard, ignore her, and get through it."

"Okay." Autumn replied doubtfully. She picked up her spoon and started to eat.

There were a few moments of silence, and then Jessie looked up and smiled at Autumn.

"I do have some good news for you. Your father is moving back to the rez."

Autumn grinned. "Really? When? Did he find a job there?"

"He is moving back in July. He found a construction job."

"Does Mom know?"

"Yes."

"What did she say?"

Jessie shook her head. "Not much. Tom was a little disappointed she wasn't more excited."

"He knows she's been dating other people," Autumn said.

"Yes, but he keeps hoping . . ."

"But Mom told him . . ."

"He wants her back," said Jessie.

"But she doesn't want that. At least not right now. And she's happy. I don't want anything to change that for her."

Jessie sighed. "He wants her to be happy. But he misses you and Sam and wants to see you guys more often."

"So he's moving back for us?"

"Well, yes, and for your mother."

"This could be a disaster. He's going to see Mom all over town with other guys."

"I know. I pointed that out to him too," replied Jessie. "But he insists he can handle it."

"I hope so," said Autumn.

"Me too," Jessie said.

"He has a temper."

Jessie sighed. "He always has."

She stood to put her bowl in the sink, and Autumn got up to do the same. They stood there by the sink for a moment, each stuck in her own thoughts.

"Are you packed up?" asked Jessie.

Autumn nodded.

"Don't worry, honey. Everything will be all right."

Autumn shook her head. "I don't know."

Jessie pulled her into a big hug and Autumn sighed, gathering her aunt close.

"I wish I didn't have to go home," she muttered, and Jessie smiled.

"You can't hide out here forever."

"Yes, I can."

Jessie laughed and then pulled away. "I love how much you've grown up in the past several months. Let's go watch some TV and relax. I think we should get to bed early. Your father will be here at seven."

"Is Ryan coming over?"

Jessie shook her head. "He's on call tonight. He said to tell you he enjoyed meeting you and hopes to see you again soon."

"I like him."

"Me too."

"So why don't you marry him?"

"Autumn . . ."

"Okay, I'll back off. But he's really cute."

Jessie laughed. "Go watch TV. I will make some popcorn and be in there in a minute."

Jessie watched her niece grab the remote and settle herself on the couch. Then she turned and headed back into the kitchen, pulling out the microwave popcorn.

Autumn was right. Ryan was a good-looking man, and she did love him. It was probably about time she settled down and started her life with him.

She smiled as she put the popcorn bag in the microwave and shut the door. She closed her eyes and sighed as she leaned against the counter.

"I wonder how Autumn would look in a bridesmaid dress," she said to herself out loud, and Autumn shrieked with excitement from the living room.

"I heard that!" Autumn called out, and Jessie shook her head and smiled.

CHAPTER 5

Here Comes Trouble

Autumn pulled on a pair of jean shorts and a T-shirt, then brushed her hair. She had to be at her tutoring class in an hour, and today she would be walking to the school and back. Her mother had to work, and a neighbor was taking care of her brother, Sam.

Autumn had been pleasantly surprised when she came home after her visit with Aunt Jessie. Her mother had deep cleaned the house, painted Autumn's bedroom a beautiful lavender color, and changed out Sam's crib for a bed. Sam loved it, but there was no keeping him in it for very long. He would lie down for a nap but got up and wandered around as soon as he was awake. Privately, Autumn thought it might have been a little early to change out the beds, but her mother didn't seem to mind chasing her son around the house.

Finally ready to go, Autumn pulled the front door open, stepped outside, and started her trek to the school several blocks away. It was times like this she wished she had a car.

As she walked, her mind drifted back to the conversation she'd had with her father on the drive home from Aunt Jessie's. Her aunt must have told him about the boy Autumn met in the office, because he spent most of the time on their trip back to the reservation advising her on the rules of dating.

Basically, he felt she was too young to date. Autumn had sat in stony silence as her father told her it would be a few years before she would be allowed to go out with boys. Autumn said nothing, realizing that her mother would be more lenient. It was best to keep that information to herself, though. She didn't want her father ruining her chances with the new boy.

Not that she had a chance with him. She had never approached him, and he seemed too shy to approach her. Even if he did talk to her, what would she say? She didn't have many friends, and she lacked the social skills to know how to handle anything that even remotely resembled a conversation with a boy.

She sighed as her gaze shifted to the school up ahead. This was the third day of tutoring, so Autumn already knew what the schedule would be for the next several hours, and it did not include goofing off. She had no idea tutoring could be so hard and wondered again how she would get through the day with Sydney glaring at her silently from across the room.

The first couple of days had been filled with tests to determine exactly what level she was at and how the school could best help her. Today would start the real tutoring, and she wasn't looking forward to it.

Autumn entered the classroom and immediately noticed two things. First, the new boy was there, and he looked up when she came into the room. He gave her a wide smile and looked at her with interest. Autumn nodded and quickly looked away, embarrassed for a moment.

The second thing she noticed was that Sydney was missing. Autumn quickly scanned the room, but the girl was nowhere in sight. Breathing a sigh of relief, she sat down in her usual chair, dropping her backpack on the floor next to her.

The teacher wasn't in the room yet, so Autumn leaned over to open her backpack and take out her pencil and notebook. When she straightened back up, the new boy was standing next to her.

"You're Autumn, right?" he asked, shoving his hands in his pockets.

She froze as she stared into his deep-blue eyes. She tried to form some intelligent words with her mouth.

"Uh . . . um . . . yeah, I am."

He nodded and then sat down at a desk across the aisle from her. "I'm Adam. The teacher said you're good at math. She thought maybe you could help me out." He stopped and looked away. "School is harder here for some reason. I mean, it seems to be." He looked back at her. "At my old school, we hadn't gotten quite as far in math as here. I need to catch up or they are going to hold me back." He looked away again. "That ain't gonna happen," he muttered, and Autumn nodded.

"I understand." When he glanced at her, she added, "I have dyslexia. I didn't tell anyone I was having issues until the end of last year, and it was almost too late." She sighed, looking down at the floor. "If I don't get my act together now, they're going to hold me back too."

He nodded then. "Is it all right if I move my stuff over here? It will be easier to work together. And I'm doing okay in English. Maybe I can help you."

"Okay."

Autumn watched him get up and gather his things, moving them across the aisle from her. Other kids entered the room, and pretty soon it was filled up. It wasn't until the teacher entered that Sydney burst into the room.

"I'm sorry," she stammered, her backpack hitting the floor as she dropped it. "My dad was supposed to bring me, but he forgot and . . ."

"Never mind all that," interrupted the teacher. "Just go sit down. We're about to start."

Sydney looked around the room and noticed the only empty chair was on the other side of the room from Autumn. Her eyes narrowed as she saw the new boy sitting across from her.

"Can I have permission to move a chair next to Autumn?" asked Sydney, picking up her backpack again. "We're supposed to be tutoring each other."

"Fine. But do it quickly. We have a lot to cover today."

Sydney picked up her chair and moved it next to Autumn just as the teacher started to talk about the work she wanted done. Then she dropped her bag on the floor again and plopped into the chair, giving Adam a smile. The teacher glared at her from the front of the room but kept talking.

Adam ignored Sydney and looked away. He knew the girl had a thing for him, but he didn't care. He only had eyes for Autumn, and he was bound and determined to get to know her better.

He glanced over at Autumn and saw her looking straight ahead, trying to ignore Sydney.

He caught her eye and smiled, and she blushed, looking away.

Satisfied at her reaction to him, he gave his full attention back to the teacher, missing the look Sydney gave to both him and Autumn.

So that's the way it is, huh? Sydney pushed her hair behind her shoulder and straightened up. There was no way Autumn was going to get her mitts on anyone she had set her sights on. The new boy was as good as hers, and Autumn had better back off.

Autumn glanced over at Sydney to see her scowling at her. What could she have possibly done now? She hadn't even spoken to the girl. With a sigh, Autumn tried to focus on the teacher.

A little while later, her stomach started to grumble. She glanced down at her watch and was surprised to see that a whole hour had already gone by.

Then a thought hit her, and she groaned to herself. Darn it, she had forgotten her lunch. Now it really *was* going to be a long day. Autumn slumped in her chair, resting her chin in her hand with another sigh.

First it was Sydney, and now she had no lunch. She hated life sometimes.

Unexpected Advice

Since Autumn had forgotten her lunch, the teacher shared some of her food with her as they worked together through the lunch period. Out of the corner of her eye, Autumn could see Sydney and Adam talking. Every once in a while, he would glance over at her, but Autumn pretended not to notice.

"Keep your eyes on the work," the teacher scolded, and Autumn nodded, going back to the English lesson the teacher had prepared for her.

"How is it going with Sydney?" asked her teacher a few moments later.

Autumn glanced up to see the teacher had removed her glasses and was rubbing her eyes.

"Ah . . . fine. Everything's fine," Autumn answered hesitantly.

The teacher put her glasses back on and regarded Autumn quietly for a moment.

"I'm new here, but I was told about her bullying you last school year. I hope that is not going on anymore."

"Did you know about that when you put us together as a tutoring team?" Autumn asked.

The teacher nodded. "Your mother told me. She wanted you paired with someone else, but I thought better of it."

"Why?"

"I always find it best to meet these things head on," the teacher said.

"Oh, I see."

"Do you?" asked the teacher.

"Not really."

"You can't run from your problems, Autumn."

"I tried telling her to leave me alone, but it never worked," replied Autumn, setting her pencil down.

"Bullies can read fear wherever they see it."

"What does that mean?" asked Autumn.

"Fear can be found in your eyes, in the way you hold yourself, and in your voice. It makes a bully feel powerful to be able to control a situation." The teacher glanced over at Sydney.

"I'm sure you heard she has family problems," she added. "She probably doesn't have much control over things at home."

"But she's been after me for years," protested Autumn. "Her parents just split up now."

"Yes, but how long have things been bad at home? Marriages don't end in a day."

When Autumn didn't reply, the teacher sighed.

"Look, it's not really my place to be talking to you about Sydney's personal life. What I'm trying to get across to you is that you have no idea what is going on in another person's life unless you've walked a mile in their moccasins."

"That doesn't excuse bad behavior."

"No, but it can explain it. You know she wasn't born that way. People can be made to feel angry and bitter. That's when they lash out at others."

Autumn sighed. "I guess."

The teacher smiled at her as she stood up. "Your mom told me that she and your father aren't together anymore," she said. "Maybe you can understand how Sydney is feeling."

"Yes, but I'm not bullying other people," Autumn pointed out.

"True," replied her teacher. "Everyone deals with things differently. How are you dealing with it? It has to be tough on you."

She held Autumn's gaze until the girl finally looked away.

"Just cut her some slack," she advised. "Everyone deserves a break." She put a hand on Autumn's shoulder. "And if that doesn't work, ignore her. Bullies hate that. No audience."

Autumn chuckled as the teacher looked up to address the class.

"All right," she said, "it's time to clean up from lunch and get back to work in your tutoring pairs."

Autumn gathered her stuff and went back to her desk, where Adam and Sydney had eaten their lunches. Adam smiled at her, and she smiled back. Sydney noticed and slipped her thermos into her backpack, dropping it noisily back on the floor.

"You seemed awfully cozy up there with the teacher," she said. "What were you two talking about?"

Autumn was half tempted to tell her to mind her own business, but another thought occurred to her.

"You," she replied, turning to look at her. "We were talking about you."

"All right, class, I need everyone's attention on me," said the teacher. "I've changed my mind. We're going to do a pop quiz in both math and English. I want to see what level everyone is at. Spread out from each other."

The students groaned, and Sydney leaned forward to whisper to Autumn.

"Me? What was she saying?"

"Sydney, there's no talking while we're testing," stated the teacher. "Come and sit up here, please."

"But Autumn told me you guys were talking about me," protested Sydney. "I was just asking what was said."

"If you want to know, ask *me*. Leave Autumn alone. Is that clear?"

"But . . ."

"Sit up here, Sydney. Move all your stuff with you."

Sydney's eyes narrowed as she gathered up her things and made her way to the front of the room. As she was setting down her backpack, she glared at Autumn.

Autumn caught the teacher's stern look and grimaced. She probably shouldn't have told Sydney they were talking about her.

Several hours later, Autumn cleaned up her desk and zipped up her backpack. Tutoring was done for the day, and she was tired.

"Hey, Autumn, I want to ask you something."

She looked up to see Adam standing in front of her with his red backpack slung over his shoulders.

"What?"

He nodded his head toward the door. "Let's go. We can walk and talk, okay?"

"I guess so."

Sydney saw what was happening and headed straight for them. The teacher glanced up from her papers and saw what was going on. She gave Autumn a nod.

"Sydney, please stay after for a few minutes," she said, motioning the girl over to her. "I would like to discuss your grade on the pop quizzes."

Sydney gave an irritated sigh, and Adam took that moment to grab Autumn's arm.

"Let's go," he said, "before she tries to follow us."

Adam led a surprised Autumn out the classroom door and down the hall. Autumn stopped and frowned at him.

"You know she likes you, right?"

He nodded, then pushed the door open and stepped outside into the sunshine. Autumn followed reluctantly.

"She's all right," he said.

"She's very pretty."

He nodded. "Yes, but I don't like the way she treats you."

Autumn bit her lip and looked away.

"Come on. Let's take a shortcut through here," he said, pulling her into Mrs. Mengen's yard.

"You can't cut through here. She doesn't like people cutting through her yard."

"It's okay. I know her."

"You do? I thought you just moved here."

"I did."

"Then how do you know her?"

"She's my grandmother."

"Your grandmother?" Autumn stopped and eyed him suspiciously. "I didn't think she had any children, let alone grandchildren. No one ever visits her. If she's your grandmother, why didn't you ever visit her?"

He shrugged. "She and Mom didn't get along. My father left us right after Mom had me."

He shook his head, studying the ground. "Mom lost her job a few months ago. She couldn't find another one, so we came here."

"Where do you live now?"

"Here. With Grandmother."

"So we are in your yard right now?" Autumn looked around her, noting the little flower bed with white petunias in it.

He nodded.

"But where are we going? I have to get home."

"I know. I'm walking you there."

"How do you know where I live?"

"I don't."

"Then how do you know we're going the right way?"

"I don't."

Autumn laughed and Adam grinned.

"You don't have to walk me home," said Autumn.

"I want to."

"Why?"

He shrugged. "Because I like you." He gazed into her eyes. "Is that okay?" he whispered.

"I don't know."

"Well, that's honest. Can I still walk you home?"

Autumn nodded shyly and watched him go to the back door and drop his backpack on the step. Then he came over to her and reached out to take hers.

"What's your Native name?" he asked, shouldering her bag.

"Dagwaagin."

"Fall?"

"Yeah, you know . . . Autumn . . . Fall."

"I see."

"What's yours?" she asked.

"Makoons."

"Bear Cub?"

He nodded. "My grandmother named me long ago."

"What happens when you grow up?"

"I'll probably get a new name. Come on, let's go."

She nodded, and together they cut through the rest of the yard and headed down the road, talking and laughing. Neither noticed a blue curtain in the window of Grandmother Mengen's house flutter open and then shut. A moment later, the back door opened and a hand reached out to pull the backpack into the house. Then the door shut quietly with a click.

Deep-Blue Eyes

Her mother's car was not in the driveway when Autumn came up the steps to the little house. It was a twenty-minute walk home from school, but talking with Adam made the time go fast. She wondered if he would realize there was no one else home and would want to come in.

"Well, this is it," she said, stopping outside the door. Adam handed her backpack to her and shoved his hands in his pockets.

"Do you want to go out sometime?" he asked. "We could take in a movie."

"Do you drive? Mom doesn't like me home after dark."

"Yeah. I got my license before we moved."

"Where did you move from?"

"Bemidji."

"Did you like it there?"

"Yeah. I left some good friends behind."

"I'm sorry."

"I was, too, until I met you."

Autumn looked away, tongue-tied and blushing.

Adam laughed. "Haven't you ever had a boyfriend before?"

"No."

"Well, you have one now, if you'll have me."

Autumn smiled. "You're moving too fast. We just met."

"Mom says if you see something you want, go after it."

"But you don't even know me."

"I know enough to like what I see. Do you have any bad habits you want to tell me about?"

Autumn laughed. "No."

"No you don't have them, or no you aren't going to tell me about them?"

Autumn laughed again, and Adam grinned.

"You're funny," she said, and he nodded.

"It's one of my better traits," Adam said.

"Maybe you should tell me what *your* bad habits are."

"No way. Too early. They might scare you away."

"Are they that bad?" Autumn asked.

"You might think so. Anyway, I'd better go now."

Adam headed down the steps and then turned around to give her another smile.

"Cut through my yard tomorrow. I'll watch for you, and we can walk to school together."

"You live right next to the school," Autumn pointed out.

"But I'm new here, and there's still a chance I might get lost," he said with a grin. "See you tomorrow."

Autumn watched him walk away for a moment and then turned and went into the house.

Her mother, Melissa, got home about five. Autumn already had supper cooking on the stove, and she took her brother, Sam, from her mother's arms as they entered the house.

"Something smells good!" exclaimed Melissa, setting down the diaper bag. "Boy, I will be glad when Sam is trained and I don't have to carry this bag around anymore."

"I made dinner," said Autumn, putting Sam down on the floor. "It's spaghetti and garlic bread."

"Thanks. I really appreciate it," her mother said. "Maybe I can grab a bath before supper. How long do I have?"

"About twenty minutes."

"I'll wait until after supper then. So how did school go today? Is Sydney bothering you?"

"Not really," answered Autumn, sitting on the couch. "But she sure doesn't like me."

"Why do you say that?"

"Well, she glares at me all the time like I did something wrong. And she hated Adam and me leaving together after school. I think she likes him."

"Who's Adam?"

"He's new. His family moved here from Bemidji."

"I see." Melissa sat down on the couch next to Autumn. "Do you like him?"

"He's nice."

"Well, that's good to hear, but what I mean is, are you interested in him?"

Autumn studied the shoes she had forgotten to remove when entering the house.

"He's okay."

"Just okay?"

Autumn couldn't help it anymore. She looked up at her mother and grinned.

Melissa laughed. "Oh, I see."

Autumn blushed and looked away.

"He's really cute, Mom. And he has blue eyes."

"Blue eyes? He's not Native then?"

"Yes, he is. Mrs. Mengen is his grandmother."

Melissa was quiet for a moment, and then she asked, "So his mother must have moved back into town then?"

"Yes, and they are living with Mrs. Mengen."

"I see."

Autumn glanced at her mother's troubled face.

"Mom, are you all right?"

"Yes, I'm fine."

"Then what is it?"

"Skye is your father's old girlfriend. They dated before we met."

"Skye?"

"Mrs. Mengen's daughter."

"Oh." Autumn thought about it for a moment and then looked at her mother again.

"Oh, I get it now. Dad's moving back, and she lives here now. You're worried they will start seeing each other again. But, Mom, you and Dad aren't together anymore, and you're dating other people."

"I know."

"But it still bothers you?"

Melissa nodded as she stood up. "I'll go check on dinner. Can you change Sam, please?"

Autumn watched her mother go into the kitchen and then picked up Sam to change his diaper.

Thinking about Adam again, she was suddenly nervous. He would probably want an answer about the date he wanted to take her on when she saw him tomorrow.

Finishing up the diaper change, she realized she was going to have to talk to her mother about the situation. She wasn't going to be able to date without permission, and her father had already said no. She'd probably get into trouble if she asked her mom about it, but she had to try. She really liked Adam.

Just then the phone rang. Her mother went to answer it, and Autumn recognized the voice on the other end. It was Aunt Jessie. She always talked too loud when she was excited.

"In the fall? I don't know. She'll already be in school," said her mother, glancing over at her. Autumn got up and headed over to her.

"Here she is," said her mother. "You can talk to her about it."

"Hi, Aunt Jessie. What? Slow down a minute. A Jingle Dress competition this fall? Oh, I don't know. I'm not that good. The play was different. I didn't dance a lot in it. When can we practice? You live in Minneapolis and I . . . No, I will be in school by then. I don't have any music. Really? Well, all right, if Mom says it's okay. I'll give you back to her."

Autumn handed the phone back to her mom. Melissa listened for a few minutes and then nodded.

"All right then, I guess that will be okay. Yes, we'll look for it. Talk to you later. Love you too. Bye."

Melissa hung up the phone and turned to Autumn. "Apparently Jessie thinks you are good enough to enter the Jingle Dress competition in Minneapolis in the fall. She is going to send you a music CD to practice with and then come for a few weeks at the end of August to fine-tune everything. Are you sure you want to do this?"

"I guess so. I mean, she seems to think I am ready. You know, I think it would be fun."

"All right then. I'll support whatever you decide. You're old enough to make some of your own decisions now. Except for this thing with Skye's son. What's his name?"

"Adam."

"That's not Native-sounding."

Autumn shook her head. "I don't think his dad is Native. That's probably who he got the blue eyes from."

"He's asked you out, hasn't he?"

Autumn looked away for a moment. "Yes."

"And you want to go?"

"Yes."

"Where is he taking you?"

"To a movie."

"I see. Well, we will have to talk about this after supper."

Autumn cleared her throat, and Melissa's eyes narrowed.

"What is it?" she asked, watching her daughter squirm.

"On the way home from Aunt Jessie's, Dad gave me a lecture about being too young to date. He wants me to wait a few years."

"A few years?" Melissa laughed. "That's too long. I think he's forgotten how old we were when we started dating."

"So then, can I . . ."

"We will discuss it after dinner," said her mother, interrupting her.

"Okay."

Autumn watched her mother gather Sam up in her arms to put him in his booster chair. She joined them at the table and smiled at her brother, who smiled back at her.

Autumn and her mother ate a quiet dinner, each in her own thoughts. With Adam and his mother back in town, it seemed that both of their lives were about to change. Autumn just hoped it would be for the better.

First Attack

As Autumn walked to school the next day, she thought about the conversation with her mother the night before. It was all right for her to go to the movie, but her mother was to drive her there and pick her up. Adam was not allowed to drive her anywhere at this point. He was a young driver, and Autumn's mother didn't want her in the car with him until he had more experience.

Autumn didn't know how she felt about the whole thing. Adam had come on a little strong the day before, and she wondered if he would end up bulldozing right over her if given the chance. He was charming and probably knew it, she reasoned. He could get a million girls, so what was he doing with her? No, she was better off just blowing him off and letting him look elsewhere for his fun. She was sure he couldn't actually be truly interested in her when the beautiful Sydney was around.

Glumly, she passed by Adam's house without noticing she had done so. He watched her from the living room picture window, frowning. She was staring at the ground and walking alone.

"I want to talk to you."

Autumn looked to her left to see Sydney heading straight for her. Autumn looked away and kept walking.

"I said I want to talk to you," said Sydney, falling in step beside her.

"What do you want, Sydney?"

"Are you and Adam going out?"

Autumn took the school steps two at a time but didn't answer. Sydney grabbed her arm before she could make it into the school.

"I know you're stupid, but are you deaf too?"

Autumn pulled away. "Go away and leave me alone."

"I will when you answer me."

"I don't want to talk to you outside of tutoring class."

Autumn turned to go, but Sydney grabbed on to her backpack, pulling it off her shoulders. Sydney threw it down the steps, and some of the contents spilled out.

Sydney took a step toward Autumn, who had silently bent down to pick up her things, when Adam appeared around the corner of the building.

He saw what was happening and ran over to the girls. Sydney grabbed Autumn's arm but dropped it when she saw him coming toward her.

"Hi, Adam," she greeted sweetly, and he nodded curtly.

"What's going on here?" he asked, watching Autumn's face closely.

Autumn wouldn't look at him.

"Everything's fine," she muttered, shoving items into her backpack. She picked it up and started through the school's double doors. Adam and Sydney followed behind her.

"Adam, there's a good movie at the cinema in town," Sydney said, taking his arm. "Want to go with me? We could grab a bite to eat afterward."

"Autumn and I are going to see the movie," Adam answered, watching Autumn. She hadn't said a word to him and wouldn't even look at him. He wondered if he had done something wrong.

Autumn turned to see both Sydney and Adam staring at her. Sydney was glaring, and Adam was watching her, frowning. She turned away and headed down the hall.

"Autumn! Wait up!"

Adam took off down the hall after her, leaving Sydney behind.

A few steps later, he caught up to her outside the door of the room where their tutoring class was held. He grabbed her arm to slow her down, but she pulled away from him. She stopped walking then, and they stood for a moment in silence, staring at each other.

"What's the matter?" he asked, shaking his head. "Why are you giving me the cold shoulder?"

Autumn didn't know what to say. Every time she was near him she became tongue-tied. She cleared her throat and looked away.

She was afraid; she knew she was. She was afraid he was just playing with her and she would end up being hurt. Suddenly she understood what Aunt Jessie had been feeling with Ryan. It took a lot of trust to let someone in, and Autumn wasn't sure she could do it.

"Autumn?" He took a step toward her. "What's wrong?" His gaze went to Sydney leaning against the lockers down the hall, watching them. "Did Sydney hurt you?" he asked her gently. "Are you all right?"

She glanced up and saw those big blue eyes watching her with concern, and she sighed.

She couldn't do it. She couldn't push him away. She wanted to. Or maybe she didn't. She bit her lip and looked away. She wanted so much to trust him.

Just then the teacher stepped out of the classroom.

"Oh, good," she said with a smile. "You're on time. Let's get started. You too, Sydney," she added, glancing down the hall.

Adam followed Autumn into the classroom, and they headed to their usual seats.

"Autumn, talk to me," whispered Adam as he set down his school bag and sat at the desk next to her. "Are you mad at me or something?"

"I can go to the movie with you," she blurted out, and instantly regretted her words.

"Really? That's great," he said, leaning back in his chair. "My first date," he added with a satisfied grin.

"Your first . . . what did you say?" Autumn frowned, shaking her head. "That can't be right."

Adam glanced at her and then looked away, slightly embarrassed. "I got permission to ask you out," he said. "My mom knows your mom or something like that. Anyway, I can go."

"You can't drive me."

"Yeah, my mom said that too. She needs the car."

"How will we get there then?"

"Can your mom drive us?"

"I can ask her."

Adam grinned. "Friday work for you? Is there a movie you want to see?"

"Not particularly. You pick."

"Okay." He sat back and then glanced at her. "I bet you've been out on plenty of dates. You're so pretty."

Autumn blushed again and shook her head. "This is my first one too."

"Really? Great! Then you can't compare me to anyone else."

Autumn gave him a shy smile, and he grinned back. The teacher picked that moment to tell them to open their books, and nothing more was said until lunch break.

Autumn pulled out her lunch and opened her drink. Adam pulled out a sandwich and started to unwrap it.

Glancing around the room, Autumn spotted Sydney. She was talking to another student, and they were laughing and pointing in her direction. The teacher had left the room, so Autumn chose to ignore her.

"Why didn't you stop at my house on your way to school?" asked Adam in between bites of his sandwich.

Autumn shrugged.

"You sure are moody," said Adam, setting his sandwich down for a swig of his drink. "My mom says girls can be that way."

"Are you and your mother close?" asked Autumn.

He nodded. "Yeah, it's always been just me and her," he said. "I have no idea where my father is."

"I'm sorry," she offered, biting into her sandwich.

"I am, too, sometimes," he replied. "But it's hard to miss what you never had."

"You never knew him?"

He shook his head. "But Mom says I got my looks from him."

"I wondered about the blue eyes."

"Yeah. It didn't matter at my old school, but around here, the guys won't even talk to me," he said glumly, setting his drink down. "I guess I don't look Native enough."

"You do," she assured him. "And I like your eyes," she added shyly.

He smiled and looked away.

Autumn got to her feet. "I have to use the restroom. I'll be right back."

Autumn was wiping her hands with a paper towel when Sydney walked in. She tried to brush past her, but Sydney stepped into her path.

Autumn sighed. "What?"

"You and I are going to have a little talk," replied Sydney.

"I don't think so." Autumn stepped neatly around her and pulled the bathroom door open as the teacher stepped inside.

Sydney opened her mouth but closed it again when she saw the teacher enter.

Autumn left immediately and headed down the hall. As she stepped into the classroom, she heard Sydney call her name. She ignored her. She went to her seat and started up a conversation with Adam just as Sydney came bursting into the classroom. Adam saw her, but Autumn kept on talking.

"So I was thinking," she said, reaching out to touch his arm to catch his attention. "If you want, we could meet and grab some extra study time. I was thinking we could go to . . ."

"You really are deaf, aren't you?" asked Sydney, striding up to Autumn. "I said I wanted to talk to you."

"I didn't feel like standing around in the bathroom talking," replied Autumn, putting her lunch away. "You know, boys don't stand around in the bathroom talking. I don't know why you do."

"That's true," said Adam. "That would be weird," he added with a laugh.

"You're just trying to make me look bad."

"Sydney, you don't need any help in that department," replied Adam. "What's your problem? Why are you giving Autumn a hard time?"

"We have something to discuss," replied Sydney, crossing her arms.

"Well, I hope it's not about me," he replied back. "I think I've made my thoughts clear about where I stand on Autumn and your behavior toward her. I like her, and you need to leave her alone, or you will have to deal with me."

Sydney watched Adam slowly get to his feet. By now, the whole classroom was watching, and Sydney could feel all eyes on her.

"I don't know why you have to bully Autumn, so knock it off. She has done nothing to you." Adam took a step toward her, shoving his hands into his pockets.

Sydney caught his gaze and went to speak, but he shook his head.

"Go sit down," he advised, "before you get into any more trouble. The teacher will be back any minute."

Sydney opened her mouth to say something, and then looked from Adam to Autumn and all the people watching her. She promptly closed her mouth again and went to go sit in her chair on the other side of the room. But that didn't stop her glare from drifting across the room.

"My hero," murmured Autumn, and Adam flashed her a smile. "But you know that might have just made things worse for me."

"I have a plan."

"Out with it."

"You are going to walk to my house every day we have tutoring and pick me up. Then I will walk you to school. I will walk you home after school too. Sydney won't be able to get near you."

The teacher picked that moment to enter the classroom.

"Okay, class, I will be passing around a piece of paper. Please put your name on it and your email address. Tutoring partners will be able to reach each other this way, and I will be able to contact you if I need to let you know something."

The teacher walked over and handed the paper to a student a few rows up from Autumn.

"We'll start on this side," she said, and Autumn shot Adam a glance.

"There is more than one way to bully someone," she said quietly. "How are you going to stop her from harassing me on social media?"

He shook his head and sat back. There was no way he was going to let anyone hurt Autumn. He would just have to think of something, and quick.

CHAPTER 9

Old Friends

T hat afternoon, Autumn's dad, Tom, was coming out of the store when he caught a glimpse of a familiar face.

"Skye? Is that you?"

Skye shut the door to her car and turned around, shouldering her purse.

"Tom! How are you?"

"I'm good. What are you doing here?"

"I live here now. We moved back a few weeks ago."

"We?"

"Adam and me. My son, Adam, I mean."

"I see." Tom replied.

"What about you?" Skye asked.

"I live in Minneapolis," Tom answered, "but I'm moving back in a week. I found a job here."

"Really? Work is hard to come by these days."

"Yeah, I was really lucky. A friend of mine was hiring, and he gave me a job."

"So you're moving back to work here?"

"Yes, and there are other reasons," Tom answered.

"I'm sorry to hear about you and Melissa," Skye said.

"Thanks. Our kids are here, and I miss them. They're part of the reason I'm moving back."

"And Melissa?" Skye asked.

Tom shrugged. "She's seeing other people."

"I'm sorry."

"Yeah, me too."

"Well, I'm looking for work. I lost my job and couldn't find another one. I had to move back home," said Skye.

"I bet that was a hard decision," replied Tom. "You and your mother never got along very well."

"She didn't like me marrying outside the culture."

"My parents weren't thrilled about it either, but Melissa and I did it anyway." Tom looked away and sighed. "Maybe they were right."

"Seems we have a lot in common," Skye said, and he smiled.

"We always did. Hey, do you want to grab a burger and catch up? I have to go talk to my new boss right now, but I could meet you in about an hour."

She gave him a smile. "Sure, that would be great. Want to meet downtown at that place we used to go to?"

Tom nodded, and Skye laughed.

"I can't believe that place is still in business," she said.

"Yeah, nothing ever changes around here. See you later."

Skye watched him walk away with a smile on her face. He was still as handsome as she remembered.

As she entered the store, she faltered for a moment.

If things worked out, she could be dating the father of her son's crush and Melissa's ex-husband. This could all end badly for everyone involved.

She pulled her phone out of her pocket to look up a number. She hoped she could find it.

Just then, the phone rang in her hand.

"Hello?"

"Hi. Is this Skye?"

"Yes. Who is this?"

"This is Melissa, Autumn's mom."

"I was just looking for your number to call you."

"Well, I wanted to talk with you about Autumn going to the movies with Adam."

"Oh, um . . . yes," Skye said. "Thanks for calling about that. Are you okay with it?"

"I think so. I told Autumn I would drive them there and pick them up."

"That would be fine," said Skye.

"You're living with your mother, Mrs. Mengen, right?" asked Melissa.

"Yes, for the time being anyway. I had to move back home when I lost my job in Bemidji."

"I'm sorry to hear about the job," said Melissa. "I will be there about six-thirty on Friday to pick Adam up."

"Sounds good." Skye hesitated and sighed.

"Is something wrong?" asked Melissa. "I can pick him up later if you think that's too early."

"No, that's all right," answered Skye. "Ah, I happened to see Tom today."

"You did? I didn't know he was in town."

"I guess he had to meet with his new boss," Skye said.

"I see."

"Look, Melissa, he asked me out. I didn't know how things were with you guys."

Melissa was silent for a moment. "I figured he would do that. He has always liked you. I have been dating other people, and we have not gotten back together. It's not like I have a claim on him."

"Will it be too weird if we happen to start dating again?"

"Probably, but go ahead. It's okay," Melissa answered.

"Thanks. And six-thirty will work just fine," Skye said. "I will send some money with Adam. Autumn won't have to bring any."

"Sounds good. Talk to you later then."

Skye hung up and shoved her phone into her back pocket. She grabbed her shopping list out of her purse and got a cart. She'd better hurry if she was going to meet Tom in an hour.

Tom arrived early to the restaurant and was already seated when she got there. After shopping, she had to go back home and drop off the frozen food before heading over to the burger joint. It made her a few minutes late.

"Hi," she said, slipping into the chair across from Tom. "Have you been waiting long?"

"Not really."

He handed her a menu, and the waitress came and took their order. Tom took a drink of his water and then toyed with the glass.

"So what have you been up to since you moved back?" he asked.

"Well, I have been out every day pounding the pavement trying to get a job. The sooner I move out of my mom's house, the better."

He nodded. "I understand that. How old is Adam?"

"He's the same age as Autumn. You know, he asked her out."

"What? How did that happen?"

"Well, they are both in a tutoring class this summer, and I guess he walked her home one day and asked her then."

Tom sat back in his chair and shook his head. "Autumn is too young to date. I told her it would be a couple of years before I would allow that."

Skye smiled. "Huh. Well, no one told Melissa that. She said it was okay for them to start dating. She's even driving them to and from the movie."

Tom sat up and leaned forward. "What? When is this happening?"

"Friday night."

"You're kidding. So Autumn went to her mom and asked if she could go out with Adam after I told her she couldn't date yet."

Skye shrugged. "I have no idea how everything went down. All I know is they are going out Friday."

"Over my dead body," declared Tom. "Excuse me a minute. I'm going to call Melissa. I'll leave a message. She's probably at work."

Tom got up and walked outside. Skye got a refill on her iced tea while she was waiting for him.

Glancing out the window, she could see Tom talking to someone on his phone. He looked upset, and he was yelling so loud, she could catch a word or two. A few minutes later, he hung up and strode into the restaurant. He pulled out his chair and sat down hard, sending Skye an apologetic look.

"Sorry I was so long," he said. "I didn't think I would be able to reach her, but she was home."

"That's all right," replied Skye, taking a sip of her drink. "What did she say?"

"She told me that while she appreciates my concern, Autumn lives with her and would follow her rules. Apparently I have no say about it."

"Ouch. I'm sorry about that. It must have been hard to hear."

"Yeah." He sighed and looked away. "It turns out Autumn did tell her I had talked to her about dating, but Melissa feels Autumn is old enough to date, so she's letting her go."

"I see."

"When I objected, she said I didn't live there anymore. She said that she has her rules, and when I get my place, Autumn will have to follow my rules when she stays with me, and she would have nothing to say about it."

Skye didn't know what to say to that, so she picked up her glass and took another drink. She secretly felt Melissa was right, but saying that out loud would not be a good idea.

"So now what?" she asked.

"I have to let it go. I can't do anything about it," Tom answered.

"Can you let it go?"

Tom sighed. "I don't know. I hope Autumn has been brought up well enough not to put herself in any compromising situations."

"Wait, are you saying my son would force her to do something against her will?" Skye set her glass down as her eyes narrowed.

He saw the look she was giving him and shook his head.

"You know, I haven't even met the young man, but I'm sure you raised him right." He sighed. "Please don't pay any attention to me," he said. "I'm just a crazed father realizing his daughter is going to start dating."

Skye relaxed and settled back in her seat.

"She's my little girl," he said sadly, picking up his glass to drink from it. "She's growing up, and I hardly see her. Pretty soon, she'll be out the door and down the street."

Skye gave him a smile. "She'll always be your little girl."

Tom shrugged.

"The divorce must have been hard on you," commented Skye.

"It is the stupidest thing I have ever done. I lost my family."

"I'm sorry. Do you still want Melissa back?"

"Yeah, but that's not going to happen. She's moved on. She's dating other people."

Skye sat back to think for a moment. She really liked Tom, but he was definitely not ready to get involved with anyone but Melissa. She must have misread his signals earlier.

Their food came, and they talked about high school and their plans for the summer. Once Skye understood that he was just interested in a friendship with her, she accepted it and relaxed. Tom relaxed, too, and pretty soon they were laughing about some high school antics when he got caught smoking behind the gym.

"Do you still smoke?" she asked.

He shook his head. "I never did. I just wanted to hang out with the cool guys."

Skye laughed and patted his hand. "I guess we all did some stupid things in school." Tom smiled at her and squeezed her hand, and that's what Melissa and Autumn saw as they entered the restaurant.

A Mending Heart

The Friday date went off without a hitch, and Autumn was now standing in front of Melissa, asking if she would take her and Adam to Strawberry Lake the following weekend. It was supposed to be hot outside, and Autumn pointed out that it might be a great way to cool down.

Melissa was hesitant after what she had seen at the restaurant. She wasn't looking forward to the possibility of seeing Skye again after she saw her holding hands with her husband.

Ex-husband. He was her ex-husband. Melissa shook her head. That was an interesting mistake to make. Did she want him back? She originally didn't think so, but now she wondered.

Looking into Autumn's hopeful eyes, she sighed and gave her a smile. Autumn seemed happier these days, and she knew it had to be because of Adam.

He had shown himself to be a respectful young man. When he called, he kept it short, and he walked her home every day and left her at the door. Autumn said he hadn't seen the inside of the house, and she believed her.

"Mom?"

Melissa nodded. "Yes, we can go to the beach. Give Adam a call and see if he can go."

Autumn's face lit up as she rushed to the phone. Minutes later she returned to the living room where her mother was sitting on the floor, folding clothes.

"He can go. I told him we would pick him up around ten. He said his mother would pack a nice lunch for us if we could pick up the drinks."

"Of course," replied Melissa, not looking at Autumn. She didn't want her daughter to see the troubled look on her face.

"Mom?"

"Yes, honey?"

"Is everything all right?"

"Yes."

"You're acting kind of weird. Is it because we saw Dad holding hands with Adam's mom?'

"He's free to do whatever he likes, honey," her mother replied, stacking Sam's laundry. "I have no claim on him."

"Just his heart."

Melissa looked up in surprise. "What?"

"Daddy still loves you."

Melissa stared for a moment and then sighed. "I know. I still love him too. But some people aren't meant to be together."

"Why? I mean, if you love each other . . ."

"Autumn," replied her mother, effectively cutting her off, "we tried to make it work. At some point you have to let go and back away."

Autumn sat down on the couch and stared off into space for a moment. Then she shook her head.

"I can see why you guys backed off," she said, "but no one has let go."

"Of course we did. We're divorced."

"Not the same thing."

"Autumn, I think you're a little too young to be making judgments about other people's relationships."

"I'm growing up, Mother. When are you going to see that? Look, I'm no dummy. I can see how you and Daddy are dancing around each other, no one wanting to approach the other one first. This is stupid."

"Are you calling your dad and me stupid? Autumn Dawn, that is disrespectful."

"Look, none of the adults in my life can move. You're all just sitting there letting good things pass you by."

"What are you talking about now?"

Autumn stood up and started to pace the room.

"Aunt Jessie could be engaged to a really nice guy, but she's dragging her feet. He's not going to wait forever." She stopped in front of her mother. "And Daddy wants you back. He's told me over and over again how stupid he was to let you go. You are just skipping through life with no concern about what anyone around you is feeling. Don't you think Sam and I want our dad back? And you still love him. It bothers you that he's dating Adam's mom." Autumn plopped back down on the couch. "I just don't understand all this. It just seems so simple to me."

Melissa stood up with the clothes in her arms and started to walk out of the room. A moment later she stopped, not turning around.

"You don't understand. He hurt me. He said some awful things about me and . . ." She stopped as a tear started to slip down her face. "I don't know if I can forgive him for that."

Autumn stood up and walked over to her.

"Mom, look at me."

Melissa turned around, and Autumn could see that she was upset.

Autumn sighed. "You and I had some bad times in the last couple of months. We said things that hurt each other. But we have forgiven each other and moved on from it."

"I know," Melissa replied, "but I don't know how to do that with your dad."

Autumn shook her head. "Life's not easy. But the best way to forgive someone is to just do it."

Melissa reached out a hand to touch her daughter's face.

"I guess you really are growing up. How did you get so wise?"

"Good parents," Autumn said.

Melissa dropped the clothes then and wrapped her arms around her daughter. They held each other for a moment before Melissa pulled away. She wiped a tear away as she bent down to pick up the clothes. Autumn bent down to help.

"Call him, Mom," she whispered. "It's time. Don't wait until it's too late."

"I'm afraid," said Melissa.

"So is he."

Melissa stared at her daughter for a moment and then nodded. Autumn watched her drop the clothes back on the couch and go to the phone. A moment later, her father picked up, and Melissa smiled. Autumn nodded at her and went to her room.

As she sat on the bed, she could hear her mother laughing. A piece of Autumn's heart shifted and slowly moved back into place. She could feel her heart mending.

No matter what came out of all this, she hoped her mother's would start mending too.

CHAPTER 11

First Kiss

Adam sat next to Sam to help him put sand into his blue bucket with his little plastic shovel. Every now and then a gentle wave would wash over them, and Sam would squeal and laugh.

Autumn watched them from the beach blanket her mother had laid out for all of them to sit on. A bright-green cooler sat behind them holding pop and juice. Her mother sat next to her, watching the boys too.

"I like him," said her mother, referring to Adam. Autumn smiled.

"Me too."

They sat in silence for a while and then Autumn reached over to grab two cans of pop out of the cooler. She handed one to her mother and then opened hers, taking a long drink.

Her mother reached into her big flowered beach bag and handed Autumn some sunblock.

"Can you put this on my back?" she asked. "You know how easily I burn."

Autumn took in her mother's fair complexion and nodded.

"Okay. Should I put some more on Sam too?"

"It couldn't hurt."

Autumn finished up with her mother and then sauntered down to the boys. Soon the water was lapping at her feet, and she stopped and closed her eyes.

Autumn loved the water. It felt good on her skin, and she loved the breeze that came off the lake. She would sit by the water all day if she could. It cleared her mind and soothed her soul.

"Autumn?"

She opened her eyes and glanced down at Adam, who was watching her.

"Mom wants sunblock on Sam," she said, plopping down next to them. She opened the tube and started slathering the thick lotion all over her brother. Adam lifted the little guy up so she could get his legs and lower back.

"It's waterproof," she said when Adam glanced at the waves headed their way.

"I figured," he said, "but a boat just went through. I think we're about to get bigger waves. Maybe we should move Sam farther up the beach."

Adam picked up the bucket and shovel as Autumn picked up Sam. He cried for a moment, not wanting to be moved, but when Autumn pointed at the waves that were now crashing onto the shore, he quieted, sticking his thumb in his mouth.

Melissa got up and took Sam from Autumn.

"Why don't you two go swimming for a while? I'm going to give Sam some juice and a snack."

"Okay, Mom," said Autumn.

The two headed down to the water. Adam stopped for a moment when he was waist deep, letting his body get used to the cold water, but Autumn pushed right through and dove straight in.

She came up laughing and sputtering. When she saw Adam still hesitating, she began wading toward him with a gleam in her eye.

"Oh, no you don't," he said, his eyes narrowing. "There will be no splashing and no pushing me under the water."

"Of course not," replied Autumn innocently, but the gleam was still in her eye.

Thinking that diving under the water on his own would be safer than anything Autumn had planned, he took a deep breath and dove in. He opened his eyes, saw Autumn's legs, and reached out to grab them, pulling her under.

Taken off guard, Autumn pushed him aside and kicked her way up to the surface.

"Gizhiikwazhiwe," she said, grinning. "You're a fast swimmer."

"I always have been," he answered. He stared at her for a moment, looking at her black hair slicked back and water dripping down her face. He smiled.

"Miikawaadizi."

Autumn blushed and looked away. He thought she was beautiful.

Her eyes dropped to the water. "Thank you," she murmured, and he smiled.

Adam hesitated a moment and then glanced back at the shore. Melissa had laid Sam down on the blanket with her back to them.

Adam turned back to Autumn, who was staring at him.

"What is it?" she asked.

He took a step toward her and leaned over, planting his lips on hers. The kiss was fast but somehow sweet and meaningful too.

When he pulled away, Autumn took a breath and glanced at her mother, who was still busy with Sam. When she moved her gaze back to Adam, she saw that he had slipped almost all the way underwater, watching her.

"Come on," he said. "I'll race you to the pontoon dock out there."

Autumn looked to her right to see people jumping off the dock. It looked like fun, but it was really far away.

"That's a long way," she said. "Think you can make it?"

"I'm a better swimmer than you," he replied, smiling. "I'll be having lunch long before you get there."

Autumn laughed, jumped into the waves, and started swimming like mad. She had no idea where Adam was, but she was sure she was going to get to the dock before he did.

She was right. She pulled herself up on the dock as soon as she reached it and sat there watching Adam finish the trip alone.

"Are you a fish in human form?" he asked her, panting.

She shrugged. "I learned to swim at an early age."

Adam hoisted himself up on the dock next to her.

"I like your suit," he said, glancing at the bright-red one-piece.

"Thanks. My Aunt Jessie bought it for me."

"So I have a question," he said, turning to look at her.

"What?"

Just then someone brushed past Autumn to jump into the water. He bumped her and she almost fell in. Adam instinctively reached out and grabbed her just before she fell.

"Hey!" Adam yelled as the boy resurfaced.

"Sorry!"

"Yeah . . ." Adam turned to look at Autumn. "Are you all right?"

She was, but he had his arms around her, and she couldn't form any words at the moment.

His eyes narrowed as he looked her over to make sure she was all right. She looked fine— just a little red in the cheeks.

She took a breath. "I'm okay. Just a little shook up."

Her gaze moved to her mom, who had seen the incident. When her mother started to stand up, Autumn gave her the thumbs-up sign, and her mother slowly sat back down. Adam dropped his arms and pulled away a little, regarding her quietly.

"Anyway, so how much of the Native language do you know?" Adam asked. "I know your dad doesn't live with you, and your mom probably isn't teaching you a whole lot."

"I speak the language well," Autumn replied. "You'll find that to be true of the people in school too. They speak both there. What about you?"

"Mom taught me," Adam said. "Dad wasn't around."

Autumn nodded. "Must have been hard growing up without him."

"Mom never talks about him, and I never ask."

"Aren't you curious about him?" asked Autumn.

"No. He didn't want us enough to stick around. He doesn't deserve my thoughts." He glanced over at Autumn. "Are you mad at your dad for leaving?"

"Yes." Autumn sighed. "And no. While I understand the situation, it's hard for all of us. Sam cries when Dad drops us off after visitation."

Adam nodded, and they were quiet for a moment. The other kids had left, and it was just the two of them on the pontoon dock for now.

"Is Sydney bothering you?"

Autumn shook her head. "I know she has my email address, but I haven't heard a thing. It makes me wonder what she's planning."

"Let me know if she starts," he said. "I'll sic my dog on her."

Autumn laughed. "You have a dog?"

"Yup."

"When did you get him?"

"A couple of days ago. He was a stray who wandered into our yard. Mom said I could keep him. We named him Fluffy."

Autumn laughed. "Fluffy? That sounds like a cat's name. What does he look like?"

"Well, I thought he was brown all over, but after we gave him a bath, we realized he is actually a cream color. And he was so fluffy after he dried off, we decided to name him that."

"What does your grandmother think?"

Adam shrugged. "I don't know. She hardly talks to me unless she wants me to do something around the house."

"She ignores you?"

"Yes. Everyone does but you and my mom."

"Everyone?"

Adam shifted his position into sitting cross-legged.

"There were some guys playing basketball by the school, and I tried to join them. They just looked at me and walked away. All the guys do that. I'm an outsider, and I have blue eyes. I heard one of them say I'm not a true Native." He sighed and looked away. "With a white father, I guess he's right."

"My mother is white," Autumn pointed out. "We are the same."

Adam nodded. "I think that's what first drew me to you. You aren't quite as dark as everyone else, and I figured you probably weren't a hundred percent Native."

"There aren't many of those out there anymore," Autumn pointed out. "I would be willing to bet some of those other guys are in the same boat as you."

"Yeah, but they were born here."

"That's true."

Autumn noticed her mother gesturing for them to come back in.

"I think it's time for lunch," she said, slipping back into the water. "Let's go back."

They swam back and ate the sandwiches and chips Adam had brought. Twice Autumn caught Adam looking at her with a warm light in his eyes, and she blushed and looked away. She knew they were both remembering the kiss.

Melissa was watching the two with amusement and sadness. She liked Adam. Autumn was not going to be alone anymore. Since Adam had shown up, her daughter was happy and content. It made her wish for those things too.

The phone call with Tom had gone all right, but they had a lot of work to do, and she wasn't sure if it would be better to just cut her losses and move on. It made her sad to think that one day her children would be grown and gone, and she might be all alone.

She glanced over to see Autumn tossing cheese popcorn into Adam's mouth. Most of the time she missed, but once in a while she got one in, and it made them both giggle.

Melissa grinned. Well, maybe it wouldn't be too soon that her children would leave and she would be on her own.

"So, Adam," said Melissa, getting the teenagers' attention now. "What are your intentions with my daughter?"

Autumn gasped, but Adam grinned.

"I plan to marry her and move to Boca Raton," he quipped.

Melissa burst out laughing as Autumn stared at her mother.

"Mom! Why would ask him that?"

"I wanted to hear what he would say. He gave the right answer." Melissa glanced over at Adam, who was still smiling. "He said he plans to get you out of my hair and move away. Sounds good to me."

"Mom!"

Adam and Melissa laughed again, and Autumn reluctantly joined in. Sam started to laugh because everyone else was, and Autumn picked up a piece of popcorn and threw it at her mother. Melissa threw it back and all heck broke loose, with popcorn flying everywhere.

A few minutes later, Melissa started to pick up the popcorn Sam wasn't trying to get into his mouth, as Autumn turned to stare at the lake again. She closed her eyes and leaned back, letting the warm breeze move through her hair.

She was happy.

The Screaming Match

Several days later, Autumn was walking up her street and heard loud yelling coming from her house. She stopped and turned to Adam.

"I think we should stop here," she said, taking her bag from him.

"Are you sure?"

She nodded.

"You're going to be all right?"

"I'll be fine. Now go!" She pushed him back a few steps and then turned nervously toward her house where the screaming was coming from.

"I think I should stay and make sure you're going to be okay." Adam took a step toward her as something crashed in Autumn's house.

"No! Go away. I don't need you. I will be fine. Just go!"

Autumn turned and ran to the house, ashamed and embarrassed at the commotion her parents were making.

She flung the door open to find her parents at a standoff. They turned to glance at their daughter and then stepped back from each other.

"Your father was just leaving," said Melissa, her fists clenching and unclenching.

"No, I'm not."

"Do I have to call the police?" she snarled back.

"Yes, Mother," Autumn said, "let's really give the neighbors something to talk about. They're already out on the lawn staring at the house. I really don't think we've attracted enough attention."

"That's enough, young lady. Don't speak to your mother like that. It's disrespectful," said her father, taking a step toward her.

"If I'm disrespectful, I have learned it from you two," Autumn snapped back, dumping her bag on the chair next to the front door.

Tom reached out and started shaking Autumn.

"You will listen and do as we say," he shouted. "We are your parents."

"Let her go!" shouted Melissa, trying to pull him away. He twisted and knocked her aside. Then he turned back to Autumn.

"Don't you ever touch her again or you will regret it the rest of your life."

They all turned toward the doorway to see Adam standing there. He looked strong and fierce, a man beyond his years.

"You want to take your frustrations out on somebody," he said to Tom, "well, here I am."

He shook his head. "You're a piece of work. It takes a real man to push women around, doesn't it?"

"Get out of here before I call the cops," replied Tom, turning his back on him.

"Go ahead. They'll take one look at this place and figure out what's going on."

"Adam, please go," pleaded Autumn, tears running down her face.

He reached out and pulled her into his arms.

"I'll go, and you're coming with me. You'll be safer at my house."

He glanced over at her parents, who stood there staring at him. Melissa's eyes were red from crying and her hair was a mess. Tom was gritting his teeth, and he was staring at Adam.

"You can have her back when you get your act together," Adam said, and Melissa gasped. Tom took a step toward him.

"Why you . . ."

Adam pushed Autumn to the door and slammed it shut behind them. He took her hand and pulled her around to the backyard of the neighbor's house. Thankfully no one was home, and Adam stopped in the middle of the backyard and pulled her to him.

They could hear Tom yelling from the front door. Then they heard the door slam and a car start. Moments later, it revved up and went down the street.

Autumn sighed. She wiped her tears away and stepped back from Adam, who was watching her.

"I have to go home," she whispered, and he nodded.

"I know," he replied, "but not yet. Where's Sam?"

"At my mom's friend's house across town."

"Okay, let's walk to my house. We can sit and talk for a while."

"Why did you come back?" Autumn asked.

Adam stared at her for a moment and then looked away.

"You should have stayed out of all of this."

He nodded. "I know. But I couldn't."

"Why?"

He caught her gaze and stared at her for a long time.

"Because I care," he muttered. Then he shrugged. "Is that all right?"

"Adam, I think it would be best if we didn't see each other anymore."

"Why?"

"My life is really complicated right now."

"I know that. But I can help. I can be there when . . ."

"You can't rescue me all the time," she said, cutting him off. "I have to fight my own battles."

"Everyone needs help now and then," he pointed out.

"Please, Adam." She started to back away. "Please understand. I can't see you anymore. I'm not going to drag you into all this crazy family stuff. You have to stay away from me."

"No, Autumn . . ."

Adam followed her as she walked back to her house. She opened the door and closed it softly behind her, effectively shutting Adam out.

He took a few steps toward the house again, then stopped. With a sigh, he turned and walked away.

Autumn was watching him from her living room window when her mother entered the room with a garbage can.

"He's got some nerve, walking in here like that," said her mother, bending down to pick up the pieces of the broken lamp.

"Don't worry about it," replied Autumn quietly. "He won't be bothering us again."

"What does that mean?"

Autumn turned from the window with dull eyes wracked with pain.

"It means I'm not going to see him anymore. I have asked him to leave me alone."

"Why?" asked her mother.

"I'm not good enough for him. *We're* not good enough."

"That's ridiculous."

Autumn shook her head slowly and started for her room. Her mother reached out to grab her arm. A sob burst from Autumn as she pulled away.

"I care about him, Mom, enough to let him go. I can't let Adam get mixed up in this mess we call a family. You and Dad were in here screaming at each other for the whole neighborhood to hear, without any thought to how this would affect me and Sam. You two are selfish, and I don't want anything to do with either one of you right now."

Melissa's eyes flared up. "You have no right to talk to me like that."

Autumn turned to look into her mother's eyes. She had never felt so miserable in all her life. She had pushed Adam away, and there was no chance her parents would ever get back together now. She gazed at her mother with all the pain and anger she was feeling, and it brought tears to Melissa's eyes.

"As far as I can see," Autumn said quietly, "you and Dad deserve each other."

And with that, she turned and left the room.

Autumn went into her bedroom and locked the door. She took her wooden desk chair and slipped it under the door handle. Then she opened her window and the screen and slipped outside, shutting them behind her. With one last glance at the house, she turned and walked away.

A New Dawn

It took Autumn several hours to get to Strawberry Lake. The sun was low in the sky, and she knew it would only be an hour or so before it disappeared completely.

She walked out on the long dock and stood at the end. Looking down at the water, she wished she could just jump in and be done with it all, but she hesitated. There was still Sam to consider, and he didn't deserve to be left behind all alone in the middle of his parents' mess.

Sitting down and leaning against a post, she closed her eyes and sighed. At least she didn't run away this time. She had just broken free from the chaos so she could think. She knew she would have to eventually go back home.

She wondered if her mother realized she was gone. It didn't really matter. She had said some things, and her parents had apparently said some things to each other, and it was going to be hard to backtrack and fix it all. She had lost all hope that things would ever get better.

A cool breeze hit Autumn's face as she sat there thinking. The temperature was dropping to a more comfortable one, and Autumn wondered idly if she could just sleep on the dock for the night. When a mosquito bit her on the leg, she changed her mind. Minnesota was the land of mosquitoes, so no, that would not be a good idea.

Autumn got up and walked back to the beach where they had sat several days before. It seemed like a lifetime ago that she was happy, sitting on the beach with Adam as he stared at her with that warm look in his eyes.

As Autumn stood in the same spot where they had all played together, tears filled her eyes. Well, at least she had the chance to be happy, if only for a moment. She had been given a memory she could keep with her forever. In the short amount of years she had been on this earth, she had learned that pain was a part of life, and sometimes it was all you got.

"What are you doing here?"

Autumn swung around to find Sydney standing behind her. Her eyes narrowed as she took a step back.

"What?"

Sydney sighed and looked away, forgoing the usual bullying that statement would have brought on at another time.

"What are you doing here?" asked Sydney again. "You're a long way from home."

"So are you."

When Sydney didn't answer, Autumn sighed. "What do you want, Sydney?"

"Nothing from you."

Autumn nodded and then turned around to face the setting sun. Sydney hesitated, then stepped up next to her. Autumn glanced at her in surprise, but neither spoke for several minutes.

"The waves are a weird combination of noisy and peaceful, all at the same time," commented Sydney, and Autumn nodded.

"I come here quite a bit to think," Autumn answered.

"Me too," said Sydney.

Autumn glanced at her in surprise. "I've never seen you here."

"You haven't seen me here now," replied Sydney. "If anyone asks, you don't know where I am." Sydney shook her head and turned to start back up the beach. "Not that anyone cares where I am," she muttered, but Autumn caught it and turned to watch her walk away.

She sat on the sandy beach looking out at the water. The sky was orange and red as it sat on the glistening waves. She smiled and closed her eyes as another cool breeze picked up. She lay back on the sand and thought for a while about her life until, emotionally exhausted, she fell asleep.

It was too quiet in Autumn's room, and Melissa wondered if the girl had fallen asleep. It had been hours since their confrontation, and Melissa had left her alone, not knowing what to say to make things right again. She sighed as she knocked gently on the door and called out to her.

"Autumn, can I come in?"

Only silence greeted her, and a mother's intuition made her go outside to look in her daughter's window.

It wasn't closed all the way, and no one was in the room. Without a moment's hesitation, she pulled the phone out of her pocket and called Tom and then put in a call to Adam. No one had seen her.

Tom roared up the street as Adam was running up the steps of the house. Tom's eyes narrowed, and for a moment, the anger came back. He pushed it away, realizing that this was not the time and that he was responsible for almost everything that had happened earlier.

Choking on his pride, he swallowed it whole as he swung into the driveway and bolted from the car. Both Adam and Melissa eyed him warily as he approached.

"Where have you checked?" he asked, looking from one to the other. "Who did you call? Where's Sam?"

"Sam is still at my friend's house across town. They said they would keep him until we find her," answered Melissa worriedly.

Tom's gaze moved to Adam. "She left with you. Where is she?"

Adam looked down at the ground. "I tried to take her back to my house, but she wouldn't go," he replied quietly. "I followed her back here and saw her go into the house."

"Why didn't she want to go with you?" asked Melissa.

Adam shrugged. "She broke up with me. She said she didn't want me to have to deal with her crazy family stuff . . . her words, not mine," he added, seeing Tom's eyes narrow.

"Tom," said Melissa, "she said she wasn't good enough for him." As she started to tear up, she added, "We made our daughter feel not good enough."

Tom reached out for her and then flinched when she stepped back.

"Give us a minute, please," he asked of Adam. He opened the door, and he and Melissa stepped inside.

"I wasn't going to hurt you," Tom whispered, watching the tears slip down her face. "I would never do that. I know I scared you, and Autumn too. I am just so frustrated you can't see how much I love you and how sorry I am for this whole mess. I'm so angry at myself for letting you go. I just want this mess to go away."

"It's abusive, Tom, the way you use words to hurt people. And your temper is out of control." Melissa shook her head. "I can't allow you to move back here. The kids shouldn't have to deal with that. They don't deserve it." She cleared her throat and took a deep breath. "I don't deserve it."

Tom was silent for a moment, and then he nodded.

"I understand," he said sadly, turning to go. "Let's find Autumn and then I'll leave you alone." He turned back to look at her and added, "It's time to let you go. I just want you to be happy." His voice broke. "I just want my family to be happy."

"Tom, you have to get some help. The anger has got to go if we have any kind of chance."

He turned around to stare at her. "What are you saying?"

"I'm saying if you can get some help and we see some changes for the better, then we have a chance."

"You mean you'll take me back?"

"Maybe. We'll see how it all goes."

"You have things to work on too," he pointed out, and she nodded.

"I know that."

"If we are going to work on things, then will you stop dating other people?"

"That sounds fair. And you too."

"I'm not dating anybody," Tom said.

"What about Skye? I saw you, remember. At the restaurant."

"What you saw was two friends comforting each other. That's all."

"Oh."

He smiled and took a step toward her, but she put up a hand to stop him.

"Baby steps, Tom. And we are not there yet."

He nodded. "Let's go find Autumn."

They stepped back outside and saw that Adam was pacing.

"Where is her favorite place to go?" he asked. "Maybe she's there."

Tom and Melissa stared at each other for a moment.

"The lake," they both said, and Adam nodded.

"Let's go."

Tom and Melissa climbed into the rickety old truck as Adam hesitated by the door.

"Get in," said Tom, eyeing him without a smile. "And if you ever talk to me like that again, I'll box your ears."

"Yes, sir."

Adam got in as Tom gave Melissa a wink and put the truck in gear. Soon they were headed down the road.

A short while later, they pulled into the public access beach parking lot. It was getting dark. They got out and headed for the beach. There was Autumn, leaning up against a post on the long dock.

"Wait," said Adam.

Tom and Melissa stopped.

"What?" asked Melissa.

"I think I should go talk to her," Adam replied.

"You?" Tom laughed. "No way." He started to move again, but Adam reached out to grab his arm.

"She's mad at you," he pointed out and then looked at Melissa. "You too."

"But she doesn't want to see you," countered Melissa.

"She was just upset," replied Adam. "But she is truly mad at you two. Let me go talk to her. Maybe I can smooth things over before she sees you." Adam stopped and then added, "Maybe you guys could go back to the truck?"

"I don't know," said Melissa, looking at Tom.

Tom ran a hand through his hair.

"No, he's right," he conceded.

Adam watched them reluctantly walk back to the truck as he headed down the slope toward the dock. It wasn't until he hit the dock and started walking that Autumn turned around and saw him. She stood up.

"Adam, what are you doing here?" She turned back around to look at the water. "I don't want to see you anymore."

Adam reached her and stopped next to her, looking out over the water too.

"Do you know why my Native name is Bear?"

"Don't you mean Little Bear?"

"A bear is a bear. They are loving and protective. They are fierce when they have to be and cuddly the next minute." He turned to catch her gaze.

"You can push me away all you want, but I'm not going anywhere," Adam said.

"So you're going to stalk me now?"

"If need be," he teased, and she smiled.

"Pest," said Autumn.

"Protector," Adam corrected her.

"What?"

"I protect those I care about."

"I see." Autumn sighed. "I could use that," she admitted. "It sounds like we're going to be great friends," Autumn added with a smile.

Adam pulled her to him. "No, Miikawaadizi, more than that."

He bent down and kissed her, and this one melted the world away. When he pulled back, her eyes were still closed. She opened them slowly and stared at him.

"Come on," he said, pulling her with him down the dock. "There are a couple of people who want to talk to you."

Autumn pulled herself together. "My parents are here? Hey, wait. How did you know I was here?"

"I didn't. Your parents figured you'd come here. They want to talk to you."

"Well, I don't want to talk to them. Tell them to leave."

Adam stopped to pull her into his arms again.

"You tell them that. They are your parents."

When Autumn went to say something, he interrupted her.

"They are human, and they make mistakes. Like you," he added with a grin, "when you said you didn't want to see me again."

She again went to speak but he shushed her.

"Give them a chance to make it up to you. Just think what you could get out of the deal." He pursed his lips, thinking. "A new car? A good shopping trip?"

Autumn laughed in spite of herself and nodded.

"All right," she agreed. "Let's get this over with."

They headed for the parking lot holding hands. When her parents saw them, Tom tensed up, and Melissa grabbed his arm.

"He's bringing our daughter back to us," she reminded him, and he sighed and tried to relax.

They stepped out of the truck as the teenagers warily approached. Melissa reached for Tom's hand.

"We should show a unified front," she whispered, and he nodded, grateful she allowed him that. He gave her hand a squeeze.

Autumn saw her parents holding hands and stopped a few feet away.

"What does this mean?" she asked, staring at their clasped hands.

"It means I'm a jerk, and I'm sorry," answered her father. "I made mistakes, but I would never hurt you or Sam or your mother. Please forgive me."

"So if I do, what then?" asked Autumn, glancing from one parent to the other.

"We're going to try," answered her mother. "We're going to get counseling and see if we can get back on track."

"So you're back together?"

"No. But we might be someday," replied her father. He glanced at Adam, who fidgeted under his gaze.

"Someone might have implied that if I can manage to pull my head out of places the sun doesn't reach and start acting like a man and not a spoiled brat, things might work out," Tom said. He hesitated a moment and then caught Autumn's gaze. "You have a good one there," he conceded gruffly, glancing at Adam again.

Autumn looked from one parent to the other and then dropped Adam's hand.

"Daddy . . ."

Tom caught her up in a hug that told her how much he loved her and how scared he was that she had been missing. Autumn, sensing that healing was finally starting for her family, glanced over at Adam, who stood there in his quiet way, just watching.

Autumn looked at him with warm eyes, and he dropped his gaze to the ground, blushing. She walked over to take his hand, and he smiled.

Maybe everything was really going to be okay this time, she thought, glancing at her parents, who were holding hands again. Autumn turned her gaze back to Adam, who smiled back at her.

After all, she had finally found her hope, and a new dawn was on the horizon.

RESOURCES

NEUHAUS ACADEMY

neuhausacademy.org

Neuhaus Academy helps teenage and adult learners improve their reading, spelling, and comprehension skills through simple online instruction. All lessons are individually tailored to each person's specific needs so that learners can work at their own pace. The courses are always free for learners and can be customized by instructors to promote and ensure a successful outcome.

FRIENDS OF QUINN

friendsofquinn.com/for-young-adults

Friends of Quinn is an online community that connects and inspires people affected by learning differences. It offers resources, social networking, and support for young adults with learning differences and for the people who love them. The website was founded by Quinn Bradlee, filmmaker and author of *A Different Life,* a book about growing up with learning differences.

SMART KIDS WITH LEARNING DISABILITIES
smartkidswithld.org

Smart Kids with Learning Disabilities aims to educate, guide, and inspire parents of children with learning disabilities or ADHD. Its goal is to help parents realize their children's significant gifts and talents and to show that with love, guidance, and the right support, their children can live happy and productive lives.

UNDERSTOOD
for learning & attention issues
understood.org

The mission of Understood is to support the millions of parents whose children are struggling with learning and attention issues. The organization strives to empower parents and help them better understand their children's issues and experiences. With this knowledge, parents can then make effective choices that propel their children from simply coping to truly thriving.

CHILD MIND INSTITUTE
childmind.org

The Child Mind Institute is an independent national nonprofit dedicated to transforming the lives of children and families struggling with mental health and learning disorders. Its objectives are to deliver the highest standards of care, advance the science of the developing brain, and empower parents, professionals, and policymakers to support children whenever and wherever they need it most.

ABOUT THE AUTHOR

KIM SIGAFUS is an award-winning Ojibwa writer and Illinois Humanities Road Scholar speaker. She has coauthored two 7th Generation books in the Native Trailblazers series of biographies, including *Native Elders: Sharing Their Wisdom* and the award-winning *Native Writers: Voices of Power.* Her fiction work includes the PathFinders novel *Nowhere to Hide,* which is the first book in the Autumn Dawn series, and The Mida, an eight-volume series about a mystically powerful time-traveling carnival owned by an Ojibwa woman. Kim's family is from the White Earth Indian Reservation in northern Minnesota. She resides with her husband in Freeport, Illinois. For more information, visit kimberlysigafus.com.

PathFinders novels offer exciting contemporary and historical stories featuring Native teens and written by Native authors. For more information, visit: NativeVoicesBooks.com

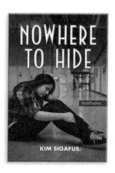

Nowhere to Hide
Kim Sigafus
978-1-939053-21-3 • $9.95

Standing Strong
Gary Robinson
978-1-939053-22-0 • $9.95

Found
Joseph Bruchac
978-1-939053-23-7 • $9.95

Trust Your Name
Tim Tingle
978-1-939053-19-0 • $9.95

Available from your local bookstore or directly from:
Book Publishing Company • PO Box 99 • Summertown, TN 38483 • 888-260-8458
Free shipping and handling on all book orders